Snowboarding

Chuck Miller

Raintree Steck-Vaughn Publishers

A Harcourt Company

Austin · New York
www.raintreesteckvaughn.com

Published by Raintree Steck-Vaughn Publishers, an imprint of Steck-Vaughn Company.

Library of Congress Cataloging-in-Publication Data
Miller, Chuck.
   Snowboarding/Chuck Miller.
      p. cm.-- (Extreme sports)
   Includes bibliographical references (p.) and index.
   Summary: Describes the sport of snowboarding and suggests how to get started as a snowboarder.
   ISBN 0-7398-4690-6
   1. Snowboarding--Juvenile literature [1. Snowboarding.] I. Title. II. Extreme sports (Austin, Tex.)

GV857.S57 M55 2001
796.93'9--dc21   2001019819

Printed and bound in the United States of America
1 2 3 4 5 6 7 8 9 10 WZ 05 04 03 02 01

Produced by Compass Books

Photo Acknowledgments
Rec Sno: title page; SD Tourism/Chad Coppess: 10, 18, 32, 34, 36, 40, 42 top, 43 top; Unicorn/Mark E. Gibson: 17, 28, 43 bottom; Unicorn/Dick Young, 30; Corbis: cover, 4, 6, 8, 12-13, 14, 20, 24, 26, 42 bottom.

Content Consultant
Gregg Davis
National Team, American Association of Snowboard Instructors

Contents

Introduction

Snowboarding is an extreme sport that is growing more and more popular. Many snowboarders ride their special boards down ski slopes. Others ride off of jumps and obstacles to do tricks.

Snowboarders look for thrills on mountain slopes around the world.

Extreme sports are relatively new sports taken up by daring athletes. Along with the fun of extreme sports, however, comes the risk of injury. People who participate in extreme sports must do everything they can to be safe.

You have probably heard of the **X Games**. But do you know what a **half-pipe** is? Do you know what a snurfer is, or how snowboarding began? Who are the top snowboarders in the world today? What do you need to do if you want to take up the sport? This book will answer all of these questions and more.

How To Use This Book

This book is divided into parts called chapters. The title of the chapter tells you what it is about. The list of chapters and their page numbers appear on the Table of Contents on page 3. The Index on page 48 gives you page numbers where you can find important topics discussed in this book.

Many snowboarders grab their boards
when doing tricks in the air.

What Does It Mean?

Each chapter has colorful photographs, captions, and side-bars. The photographs show you things written about in the book, so you will know what they look like. A caption is an explanation that tells you about the photograph. The captions in this book are in light blue boxes. Side-bars give you extra information about the subject.

You may not know what some of the words in this book mean. To learn new words, you look them up in a dictionary. This book has a dictionary called a glossary. Words that appear in boldface type are in the glossary on page 44.

You can use the Internet sites listed on page 46 to learn more about topics discussed in this book. You can write letters to the addresses of organizations listed on page 46, asking them questions or to send you helpful information.

Snowboarding

Snowboarding is a cross between surfing and skiing. Snowboarders strap a wide board to their feet and ride down snow-covered hills or mountains. A snowboard looks like a wide ski.

The two main kinds of snowboarding are **freeriding** and **freestyle**. Freeriders ride their boards down hills and ski mountains. Freestylers ride their boards on **ramps** and do tricks.

A third kind of snowboarding recognized by the American Association of Snowboard Instructors (AASI) is called Alpine, or racing. These boarders use plastic **boots** like skiers and ride on smooth, groomed trails and race through gates like ski racers.

Snowboarders can ride their boards on almost any kind of snow. The kind of snow they like best is **powder**. Powder is fresh snow that nobody has ridden on yet. It sprays into the air as snowboarders ride it.

Special boots and bindings hold a boarder's feet to his or her board.

Where Do Snowboarders Ride?

Snowboarders often ride their boards on the same slopes as skiers. When snowboarders and skiers share trails, they need to follow basic safety rules toward each other. In the past, snowboarding was not allowed at many ski resorts. A resort is a place where people go for rest and fun. Since the late 1980s, however, snowboarding has become so popular that many ski resorts have opened their trails to snowboarders.

Some ski resorts have special rules for snowboarders. A common rule is that boarders must have a **safety leash** for their boards. This ties their snowboard to their bodies. It keeps boards from getting away when boarders fall. The safety leash is mainly for step-in **bindings**, which could release when boarders are riding ski lifts. A loose board sliding down a mountain could injure another boarder or a skier. Boarders also hold the leash while walking with their boards.

Snowboarding Parks

Many ski resorts have built special parks for snowboarders. These have ramps, bumps, and jumps made of snow that snowboarders can use to do tricks.

Different Kinds of Snowboarding

Freeriding is the most popular kind of snowboarding. Almost anyone can freeride their board down hills or ski mountains.

Freeriders can ride their boards however they want, as long as they are safe. They may ride their boards straight down a mountain or hill. They may choose to use bumps on a hill to do tricks on their way down.

Freestyling is more difficult. Boarders use ramps to do tricks called **aerials**. Aerials are spins and flips done while in the air. Boarders try to jump as high as they can when doing aerials. They call this "catching air."

Snowboarders like to ride in fresh snow called "powder."

13

This snowboarder has a safety leash attached to his foot and his board.

How Snowboarding Began

In the mid-1960s, a man named Sherman Poppen attached two skis together with screws. He then tied a rope to the front and rode it down a hill. He called his invention the snurfer, a cross of the words "snow" and "surfer." Snurfing became popular in the 1960s, and Poppen sold millions of snurfers.

In the 1970s, many surfers and skateboarders tried to improve snurfers. In 1977, Jake Burton started making snowboards. They were made out of wood with a plastic bottom. The plastic helped the boards go quickly through fresh powder. He put rubber straps on the top of the boards so riders could tie them to their boots.

Burton's new boards made snowboarding popular. He started his own company, which he called Burton. Another snowboarder named Tom Sims also started making snowboards. His called his company Sims. Today, Burton and Sims are two of the most popular kinds of snowboards.

Early Competitions

In the early 1980s, Burton and Sims helped start the first snowboarding competitions. In 1988, the United States Amateur Snowboard Association (USASA) began. The International Snowboard Federation (ISF) began that year as well. These groups held snowboarding competitions and made rules for them.

In 1995, the sports television network ESPN started the Extreme Games. Today, this competition is known as the X Games, and it has become the best-known competition for all kinds of extreme sports. Snowboarders ride in several different freestyle and freeriding events at the X Games. This helped make snowboarding a popular sport that is now seen by millions of people on television. In 1998, snowboarding became an Olympic sport.

This snowboarder has caught "big air" on a slope at a ski resort.

Beginning snowboarders need to practice often if they want to ride as well as experienced boarders.

What Do I Need to Start?

Pads and guards protect snowboarders when they fall. Boarders should always wear wrist guards. Wrist guards keep a boarder's wrists straight during a fall. This way, boarders have a lesser chance of injuring their wrists. Hands and wrists are the areas most often injured in a fall.

Some snowboarders use **helmets**. In 1999, the Consumer Products Safety Commission released a report. It recommended that all snowboarders below the age of 14 should wear helmets. Because head injuries can be very serious, every beginner should wear a helmet.

The Right Clothing

Snowboarders need to stay dry and warm, so the right clothes are important. Boarders could get hypothermia if they become too cold. Hypothermia means a person's body temperature becomes dangerously low.

This experienced snowboarder is wearing clothes to stay warm and protect the skin.

Layers

Boarders can also get frostbite. Frostbite means a person's skin has been damaged by extreme cold. Snowboarders should wear several layers of loose clothes. Loose clothing lets boarders move quickly and easily. The outside layers should be made of waterproof and windproof material, such as nylon with a waterproof coating.

Boards

Freestyle boards are wide and stable, and are easier to do tricks with. Freestyle boards also bend easily, so they do not break during tricks. The nose and tail of freestyle boards are the same shape. This is so snowboarders can ride forward or backward.

Freeriding boards do not bend as easy as freestyle boards. The noses are turned up. They ride and turn easily through powder. They are not as wide as freestyle boards. Some boarders use freeriding boards to race.

Did You Know?

Did you know that some kinds of snow are better to ride on than others? Wet snow, for example, is sticky. This slows down boarders and makes it harder for them to turn.

What Safe Snowboarders Do

Snowboarders should not ride down slopes they think are too steep. Many boarders use the "falling leaf" way of riding down steep hills. They ride their boards back and forth, the way a leaf falls from a tree. They do this until they reach the bottom. It lets them go as fast or as slow as they want.

When doing ramps or jumps, boarders must always check in advance where they are going to land. They need to know if they will have to slow down or stop right after landing. They must also make sure they will not land on a flat piece of ground. They could injure their ankles if they do. An injury is some kind of hurt or damage, such as broken bones or a sprain. A sprain means one of the body's joints has been twisted, tearing its muscles or ligaments. A ligament holds together the bones in a joint.

Boarders should not ride with their boards flat on the ground. They should always keep the board on one edge or the other. If they catch an edge on a bump while riding flat, they will fall hard.

Racing Boards

Racers ride boards with a flat tail because they only go forward. Racing boards are the stiffest kinds of snowboards.

Boots and Bindings

Most snowboarders begin with soft boots that bend easily. Boots strap into the board's bindings. This keeps a snowboarder's feet on the board.

Most racers use hard boots. The hard outer shell of the boot gives support and lets them turn quickly. The boots slip into the bindings and are held with special clips.

Downhill Courses

Most freeride boarders ride downhill ski trails. They often use bumps or logs for tricks. They may drag their boards across them to do spins and turns.

Did You Know?

Did you know that one kind of snow is called corn snow? Corn snow is powder that has thawed and then refrozen. Why is it called corn snow? Because it looks like little corn kernels. Corn snow is easy for boarders to ride on.

Choosing a Snowboard

Choosing the right snowboard is necessary to ride safely and well. The wrong board used for the wrong kind of riding will not work well. It also can be dangerous.

Many snowboard makers will make boards exactly how snowboarders want them. Boarders tell the company how they will be riding. They also tell them the style and colors they would like. The length of the snowboard depends on the size of the rider.

New snowboards are often expensive. Boarders can buy used snowboards for less money. Many new snowboarders buy used boards. Most ski resorts where snowboarding is allowed will also rent boards. For young and beginning riders, renting is often a good idea, especially since they are likely to grow from winter to winter.

Boarders who leave ski trails must check out the route they will be riding to make sure it is safe.

Leaving Trails

Some freeride boarders will leave the main ski trails and ride through trees. Most snowboarders who do this have been snowboarding for a long time.

Jumps

Freestyle snowboarders use different kinds of jumps to do tricks. One jump is the **quarter-pipe**. It has one curved wall. Another jump is the half-pipe. It has two curved walls and is shaped like a "U." Freestylers try to catch as much air as they can at the top of jumps.

Some boarders want to catch more air than a quarter-pipe or half-pipe will allow. They use **big air** ramps to do tricks. These are shaped like ski jumps. Boarders ride down them and jump into the air to do tricks.

Boarder Profile: Todd Richards

Todd Richards has been a snowboarder since 1990. He was born in Worcester, Pennsylvania in 1969, and he now lives in Breckenridge, Colorado. Richards rides mainly in half-pipe competitions. He won two gold medals at the X Games between 1997 and 2000.

This boarder is using the edge of the board to make a turn across a slope.

Who Can Become a Snowboarder?

Almost anyone can start snowboarding if they are prepared. It helps to be in good shape. Before beginning, new boarders need to buy the right snowboard. They also need to learn the safety rules. Then, new snowboarders must learn how to ride.

Snowboarders use many muscles in their bodies, so stretching is important. Boarders who stretch arm, leg, and back muscles get injured less often. They feel more rested and awake while riding.

Learning to Snowboard

Boarders use two edges, one under their toes and one under their heels. They step onto their board with their body and both feet pointing toward the toe edge of the board. One of their feet is the front foot while the other is the back.

 This snowboarder is riding goofy-footed.

Regular and Goofy-Footed

Most boarders lead with their left foot while riding. Some, however, lead with their right foot. This is called riding "goofy-footed."

Boarders start moving by pointing the nose of their board down a slope. They lean forward to begin moving. They bend their knees and lean toward the edge of the board their toes face. Then they lean back, toward the other side of the board. This turns them in the other direction. Riding back and forth across a hill like this lets boarders control their speed.

Snowboarders stop much like ice hockey players do. They bring both feet around so that they are pointing across the slope of a hill. Then they scrape their boards across the snow and move across the hill to stop.

Where do I train?

Many ski resorts have snowboarding teachers who give free lessons to new boarders. Boarders should make sure their teacher belongs to the AASI. Most ski areas support AASI and provide instructors that have been trained to teach people to snowboard the best and fastest way. This group is always giving its teachers lessons on new skills and safety tips.

New snowboarders also can contact the United States of America Snowboard Association (USASA) to learn about snowboarding schools and camps. The USASA was started in 1988 by a group of snowboarders. It holds snowboarding competitions across the United States.

This snowboarder is riding a half-pipe in a competition.

Who Are the Professional Snowboarders?

Ross Powers is one of the best half-pipe snowboarders in the world. He won the bronze medal in the half-pipe at the 1998 Olympics. Powers has also won a pair of gold medals and a silver medal at the X Games. He was born in Vermont in 1979. He still lives in Vermont, where snowboarding is very popular.

Barrett Christy is another popular snowboarder. Many different sports magazines have published articles about her. She was born in Buffalo, New York in 1971, and now lives in Vail, Colorado. She rides mainly in freestyle competitions. She won four gold medals and four silver medals at the X Games between 1997 and 2000.

 Beginning boarders need to practice before trying tricks like this one.

Practice

Like anyone who wants to learn how to snowboard, Powers and Christy had to start at the beginning. They practiced easy tricks first and then learned more difficult ones. Today, they invent new tricks of their own. Like learning to ride, each new trick takes a lot of practice and hard work.

Riding the Pipe

To ride half-pipes, boarders begin by riding across the pipe to build speed. Then they ride up the wall of a pipe and jump into the air at the top. They try to jump as high as they can to catch air. Boarders who catch more air can do more difficult tricks. Boarders often grab onto their boards when doing tricks.

Big Air snowboarders begin by riding down a ski jump or ramp. They jump into the air at the bottom to do tricks. The bottom of many ramps is often more than 100 feet (30 m) above the ground. Boarders must land the right way or they could get hurt.

Timeline

1960s: Sherman Poppen invents the snurfer

1977: Jake Burton invents a snowboard

1980s: Jake Burton and Tom Sims start the first snowboarding competitions

1988: United States of America Snowboard Association begins

1998: Snowboarding becomes an Olympic winter sport

This snowboarder is riding regular-footed.

Boarder Profile: Jason Borgstede

Jason Borgstede is a well-known big air snowboarder. He won a gold medal in 1998 and a silver medal in 2000 at the X Games. Borgstede was born in St. Louis, Missouri, in 1975. He now lives in Eagle River, Arkansas.

Riding the Hill

Some snowboarders like to race. The two kinds of snowboarding race courses are **slalom** and **giant slalom**. In slalom competitions, racers ride down different courses next to each other. They use their boards to turn in and out of flags placed along the courses. The first snowboarder to reach the bottom of the course is the winner.

In giant slalom competitions, a single boarder races down a larger course as quickly as he or she can. They must make bigger and faster turns than in slalom competitions. The boarder who rides the course fastest wins.

Most snowboarders are not skilled enough to earn a living from their sport.

Competing in Snowboarding

Anyone can join the United States Ski and Snowboard Association (USSA). It holds snowboarding competitions for both new and experienced snowboarders. It also chooses boarders for the U.S. Snowboard Team. These snowboarders get to compete in the Olympics.

The USSA has held snowboarding competitions since 1988. In 1993, it united with the International Snowboard Federation (ISF). The ISF holds competitions for snowboarders from more than 40 countries.

Rankings

Professional boarders earn their living from riding. Most ride in national and international competitions year round. Boarders are ranked by how well they do. The highest ranked boarders ride in the X Games, Olympics, and World Championships.

Judging Events

Pro boarders have a set amount of time to ride pipes in freestyle competitions. Judges give points for the number of tricks they do. Harder tricks get more points. Judges also give boarders points for style and for how high they jump.

Big Air snowboarders also receive points for the number of tricks they do. Harder tricks get more points. Big Air snowboarders can also earn points for their landings.

Slalom boarders race against a clock. The boarder who takes the least amount of time to finish the course wins the race.

Competitions and Prizes

In 1998, snowboarding became an Olympic winter sport. Boarders from around the world rode in slalom and freestyle competitions. The Winter Olympics take

Did You Know?

Do you know the difference between granular snow and corn snow. Like corn snow, granular snow is powder that has thawed and then refrozen, except granular snow refreezes as a flat sheet. This makes granular snow very slippery, almost like ice.

place every four years and are held in a different country each time.

The USASA and USSA also hold many national competitions each year. The ISF holds many international competitions. All of these groups hold freestyle and slalom events.

Pro boarders also ride in slalom, freestyle, and Big Air events in the X Games. The X Games also feature a competition called the Boardercross, or snowboard cross. In it, several boarders race down a slope at the same time. They use jumps and bumps to do tricks on the way down. The first to the bottom is the winner.

Boarder Profile: Gian Simmen

In 1998, Gian Simmen became the first male snowboarder to win the gold medal in the half-pipe in the Olympics. Simmen is know for his ability to catch big air and do amazing tricks. He was born in 1977 in Switzerland, where he still lives.

Many snowboarders like to be alone on the slopes, among the natural wonders of winter.

Sponsors

A **sponsor** is a business or a person who pays for a snowboarder to ride. The sponsor pays for the boards and also for safety equipment. Some sponsors pay for boarders to travel to races around the country and the world.

Many sponsors are snowboard makers. Boarders wear each sponsor's name on their clothes and on their boards. Sponsors hope people will see their name and buy their products.

A Growing Sport

Snowboarding has become a very popular sport. Many surfers and skateboarders helped build the sport's popularity. They have taken up snowboarding in addition to their other sports. Each year, snowboarders continue to invent new and better tricks. More and more people watch snowboarding events—in person and on television—every year.

Quick Facts About
Snowboarding

Snowboarders call riding down a hill back and forth "turning."

"Carving" is when snowboarders let their boards slice through the snow while turning.

"Skidding" is when snowboarders let their boards slip sideways across the snow while turning.

Snowboarders held onto their boards with a rope before ski-style bindings were developed for snowboards.

A snowboarder's bindings are round and shaped to fit the boot. Ski bindings are much longer.

In 1985, less than half of all downhill ski areas allowed snowboarding on their hills.

Nicola Thurst of Germany won the first Olympic gold medal in the women's half-pipe.

Glossary

aerial (AIR-ee-uhl)—a trick done while catching air

big air (BIG AIR)—a type of snowboarding where snowboarders ride down a long narrow ramp to do tricks high in the air

binding (BINDE-ing)—what snowboarders use to fasten their boots to their boards

boot (BOOT)—what snowboarders wear over each foot

freeride (FREE-ride)—a style of snowboarding where people ride down a ski run or slope

freestyle (FREE-stile)—a style of snowboarding where people ride their boards on jumps to do tricks

giant slalom (JYE-uhnt SLAL-uhm)—a race down a single obstacle course, done one racer at a time

half-pipe (HAF PIPE)—a U-shaped jump with two curved walls

helmet (HEL-mit)—a hard kind of hat that protects a person's head

powder (POU-dur)—freshly fallen snow that no one has snowboarded or skied on

professional (pruh-FESH-uh-nuhl)—a person who makes money doing something others do for fun

quarter-pipe (KWOR-tur PIPE)—a jump with one curved wall that the rider lands back on

ramp (RAMP)—a curved surface used for freestyle tricks

safety leash (SAYF-tee LEESH)—a rope or cord attached to a snowboarder's board to prevent it from slipping away

slalom (SLAL-uhm)—a snowboarding or ski race down an obstacle course

sponsor (SPON-sur)—a company who pays someone to use or advertise its product

X Games (EKS GAYMZ)—a popular extreme sports competition hosted by the sports television network ESPN

Internet Sites and Addresses

American Association of Snowboard Instructors
http://www.aasi.org

About.com: Snowboarding
http://www.about.com/snowboarding

ESPN.com Extreme Sports
http://espn.go.com/extreme

International Snowboard Federation
http://www.isf.net

U.S. Amateur Snowboard Association
http://www.usasa.org

American Association of Snowboard Instructors
133 South Van Gordon Street
Suite 100
Lakewood, CO 80228

Canadian Snowboard Federation
250 West Beaver Creek Road
Unit One — Second Floor
Richmond Hill, ON L4B 1C7
Canada

Unites States of America Snowboard Association (USASA)
P.O. Box 3927
Truckee, CA 96160

Books to Read

Hayhurst, Chris. *Snowboarding! Shred the Powder.* New York: Rosen, 1999. This book introduces the sport of snowboarding, with advice for beginners on equipment, techniques, competition, and safety.

Iguchi, Bryan. *The Young Snowboarder.* London: DK, 1997. This book provides information on the history of snowboarding, necessary equipment, and step-by-step instructions on the techniques and moves involved.

Kidd, P. J. *Snowboarding: Big Air and Boarder X.* Extreme Games. Edina, Minn.: Abdo & Daughters, 1999. This book discusses the athletes and the vocabulary of two snowboarding events, Big Air and Boarder X.

Malthouse, Becci. *Extreme Sports: Snowboarding.* New York: Franklin Watts, 1997. This book introduces snowboarding moves and discusses snowboarding as an extreme sport.

Index